STORIES IN TIME

LIVING IN OUR WORLD

ASSESSMENT PROGRAM

HARCOURT BRACE & COMPANY

Orlando Atlanta Austin Boston San Francisco Chicago Dallas

New York Toronto London

ISBN 0-15-303577-3

5 6 7 8 9 10 022 99 98

CONTENTS

Overview

The assessment program in *Stories in Time* allows all learners many opportunities to show what they know and can do. It provides you with ongoing information about each student's understanding of social studies.

The assessment program is designed around the Assessment Model in the chart below. The multi-dimensional framework is balanced between teacher-based and student-based assessments. The teacher-based strand typically involves assessments in which the teacher evaluates a student's work as evidence of his or her understanding of social studies content and ability to think critically about it. The teacher-based strand consists of two components: Formal Assessment and Performance Assessment.

The student-based strand involves assessments that invite the student to become a partner in the assessment process. These student-based assessments encourage students to reflect on and evaluate their own efforts. The student-based strand also consists of two components: Student Self-Evaluation and Portfolio Assessment.

The fifth component in the *Stories in Time* assessment program is Informal Assessment. This essential component is listed in the center of the Assessment Model because it is the "glue" that binds together the other types of assessment.

STORIES IN TIME
Assessment Model
Grade 3

Teacher-Based	Student-Based

Formal Assessment
• Lesson Reviews
• Unit Review
• Unit Assessment
   Standard Test
   Performance Tasks
	Student Self-Evaluation
	• Individual End-of-Project Summary
	• Group End-of-Project Checklist
	• Individual End-of-Unit Checklist

Informal Assessment
• √ Questions
• Think and Apply
• Story Cloth Summary
• Social Studies Skills Checklist

Teacher-Based	Student-Based
Performance Assessment • Show What You Know • Cooperative Learning Workshop • Performance Task/Scoring Rubric • Scoring Rubric for Individual Projects • Scoring Rubric for Group Projects • Scoring Rubric for Presentations	**Portfolio Assessment** • Student-Selected Work Samples • Teacher-Selected Assessments • A Guide to My Social Studies Portfolio • Portfolio Summary • Family Response

Description of Assessment Components and Materials in this Booklet

Informal Assessment

Informal Assessment is central to the *Stories in Time* assessment program. Ultimately, it is your experienced eye that will provide the most comprehensive assessment of students' growth. This booklet provides a checklist to help you evaluate the social studies skills that your students demonstrate in the classroom (pages 4–5).

Formal Assessment

This booklet provides Unit Assessments (beginning on page 15) to help you reinforce and assess students' understanding of ideas that are developed during instruction. Each Unit Assessment includes a standard test and performance tasks. Answers to assessment items and suggested scores are provided in the Answer Key (beginning on page 63).

Student Self-Evaluation

Student self-evaluation encourages students to reflect on and monitor their own gains in social studies knowledge, development of group skills, and changes in attitude. In this booklet, you will find checklists for both individual and group self-evaluation (pages 6–8).

Performance Assessment

Social Studies literacy involves more than just what students know. It is concerned with how they think and do things. This booklet provides scoring rubrics to help you evaluate individual projects, group projects, and student presentations (pages 9–11).

Portfolio Assessment

For portfolio assessment, students create their own portfolios, which may also contain a few required or teacher-selected papers. Included in this booklet are support materials to assist you and your students in developing portfolios and in using them to evaluate growth in social studies (pages 12–14).

Rating Scale

3 Proficient
2 Adequate
1 Improvement needed
☐ Not enough opportunity to observe

Students' Names

Geography Skills

understanding globes					
understanding the purpose and use of maps					
comparing maps with globes					
comparing maps with photographs					
understanding map symbols					
understanding directional terms and finding direction					
understanding and measuring distance					
understanding and finding location					

Chart and Graph Skills

understanding and using pictographs					
understanding and using charts and diagrams					
understanding and using bar graphs					
understanding and using calendars and time lines					
understanding and using tables and schedules					

Other Visual Skills

understanding photographs and other picture illustrations					
understanding fine art					
understanding safety and information symbols					
understanding patriotic and cultural symbols					
understanding artifacts and documents					

Reading Skills

using context clues to understand vocabulary					
using illustrations or objects to understand vocabulary					
grouping and categorizing words (semantic maps)					
understanding multiple meanings of words					
understanding literal and implied meanings of words					
understanding root words, prefixes, and suffixes					
understanding abbreviations and acronyms					
understanding facts and main ideas					
identifying and understanding various types of text					

Research Skills

locating and gathering information					

(continued)

	Students' Names						
Thinking Skills							
identifying cause-and-effect relationships							
following sequence and chronology							
classifying and grouping information							
summarizing							
synthesizing							
making inferences and generalizations							
forming logical conclusions							
understanding and evaluating point of view and perspective							
evaluating and making judgments							
predicting likely outcomes							
making thoughtful choices and decisions							
solving problems							
Communication Skills							
writing and dictating							
speaking and listening							
dramatizing and role-playing simulations							
making observations							
asking questions							
listing and ordering							
constructing and creating							
displaying, charting, and drawing							
Citizenship Skills							
working with others							
resolving conflicts							
acting responsibly							
keeping informed							
respecting rules and laws							
participating in a group or community							
respecting people with differing points of view							
assuming leadership							
being willing to follow							
making decisions and solving problems in a group setting							

Name _____

Date _____

To Sum It Up

You can tell about and evaluate your project by completing these sentences.

1. My project was about _____

_____

2. These people helped me as I worked on my project: _____

_____

_____

3. I gathered information from these sources: _____

_____

_____

4. The most important thing I learned from doing this project is

_____

_____

_____

5. I will use what I have learned _____

_____

6. My evaluation of my project is _____

_____

I think I deserve this evaluation because _____

_____

7. I would like to say _____

_____

_____

How Did Your Group Do?

Mark the number that tells the score you think
your group deserves.

How well did your group	High		Low
1. plan for the activity?	3	2	1
2. carry out group plans?	3	2	1
3. listen to and show respect for each member?	3	2	1
4. share the work?	3	2	1
5. solve problems without the teacher's help?	3	2	1
6. make use of available resources?	3	2	1
7. record and organize information?	3	2	1
8. communicate what was learned?	3	2	1
9. demonstrate critical and creative thinking?	3	2	1
10. set up for the activity and clean up afterwards?	3	2	1

Think about each question below and write a short answer.

11. What did your group do best? _____

_____

_____

12. What can you do to help your group do better work? _____

_____

_____

13. What did your group like best about the activity? _____

_____

_____

Name _____ Date _____

Unit Title _____

Here's What I Think

Decide whether you agree or disagree with each statement below. Circle the word that tells what you think. If you are not sure, circle the question mark. Use the back of the sheet for comments.

1. This unit was very interesting.	**Agree**	**?**	**Disagree**
2. I learned a lot.	**Agree**	**?**	**Disagree**
3. I enjoyed working in groups.	**Agree**	**?**	**Disagree**
4. I enjoyed working alone.	**Agree**	**?**	**Disagree**
5. I felt comfortable giving my ideas and raising questions.	**Agree**	**?**	**Disagree**
6. I was cooperative and helped others learn.	**Agree**	**?**	**Disagree**
7. I contributed my fair share to group work.	**Agree**	**?**	**Disagree**
8. I am getting better at making decisions and solving problems.	**Agree**	**?**	**Disagree**
9. I worked on social studies at home and in the community as well as at school.	**Agree**	**?**	**Disagree**
10. I understood the ideas in this unit.	**Agree**	**?**	**Disagree**
11. I think I am doing well in social studies.	**Agree**	**?**	**Disagree**

Think about each question below and write a short answer.

12. What did you like best in this unit? Tell why. _____

_____

13. What is something you can do better now than you could do before?

_____

_____

14. What is something you understand now that you didn't understand before?

_____

_____

Name _____ Date _____

Check the indicators that describe the student's performance on a project or task. The section with the most check marks indicates the student's overall score.

4 Point Score Indicators: The student
_____ gathers a lot of relevant, accurate information.
_____ shows thorough understanding of content.
_____ demonstrates strong social studies skills.
_____ exhibits outstanding insight/creativity.
_____ communicates ideas clearly and effectively.

3 Point Score Indicators: The student
_____ gathers sufficient relevant, accurate information.
_____ shows adequate understanding of content.
_____ demonstrates adequate social studies skills.
_____ exhibits reasonable insight/creativity.
_____ communicates most ideas clearly and effectively.

2 Point Score Indicators: The student
_____ gathers limited relevant, accurate information.
_____ shows partial understanding of content.
_____ demonstrates weak social studies skills.
_____ exhibits limited insight/creativity.
_____ communicates a few ideas clearly and effectively.

1 Point Score Indicators: The student
_____ fails to gather relevant, accurate information.
_____ shows little or no understanding of content.
_____ does not demonstrate social studies skills.
_____ does not exhibit insight/creativity.
_____ has difficulty communicating ideas clearly and effectively.

Overall score for the project _____

Comments:

Group _____ Date _____

Check the indicators that describe a group's performance on a project or task. The section with the most check marks indicates the group's overall score.

4 Point Score Indicators: The group
_____ makes outstanding use of resources.
_____ shows thorough understanding of content.
_____ works very cooperatively; contributions are about equal.
_____ displays strong decision-making/problem-solving skills.
_____ exhibits outstanding insight/creativity.
_____ communicates ideas clearly and effectively.

3 Point Score Indicators: The group
_____ makes good use of resources.
_____ shows adequate understanding of content.
_____ works cooperatively; contributions are nearly equal.
_____ displays adequate decision-making/problem-solving skills.
_____ exhibits reasonable insight/creativity.
_____ communicates most ideas clearly and effectively.

2 Point Score Indicators: The group
_____ makes limited use of resources.
_____ shows partial understanding of content.
_____ works cooperatively at times, but contributions are unequal.
_____ displays weak decision-making/problem-solving skills.
_____ exhibits limited insight/creativity.
_____ communicates some ideas clearly and effectively.

1 Point Score Indicators: The group
_____ makes little or no use of resources.
_____ fails to show understanding of content.
_____ does not work cooperatively, some members don't contribute.
_____ does not display decision-making/problem-solving skills.
_____ does not exhibit insight/creativity.
_____ has difficulty communicating ideas clearly and effectively.

Overall score for the project _____

Comments:

Name _____ Date _____

Check the indicators that describe the student's or group's presentation. The section with the most check marks indicates the overall score for the presentation.

4 Point Score Indicators: The presentation
_____ shows evidence of extensive research/reflection.
_____ demonstrates thorough understanding of content.
_____ is exceptionally clear and effective.
_____ exhibits outstanding insight/creativity.
_____ is of high interest to the audience.

3 Point Score Indicators: The presentation
_____ shows evidence of adequate research/reflection.
_____ demonstrates acceptable understanding of content.
_____ is, overall, clear and effective.
_____ shows reasonable insight/creativity.
_____ is of general interest to the audience.

2 Point Score Indicators: The presentation
_____ shows evidence of limited research/reflection.
_____ demonstrates partial understanding of content.
_____ is clear in some parts but not in others.
_____ shows limited insight/creativity.
_____ is of some interest to the audience.

1 Point Score Indicators: The presentation
_____ shows little or no evidence of research/reflection.
_____ demonstrates poor understanding of content.
_____ is, for the most part, unclear and ineffective.
_____ does not show insight/creativity.
_____ is of little interest to the audience.

Overall score for the presentation. _____

Comments:

Name _____ Date _____

A Guide to
My Social Studies Portfolio

What Is in My Portfolio	Why I Chose It
1.	
2.	
3.	
4.	
5.	
6.	

I organized my portfolio this way because _____

_____

_____

_____

Name _____ Date _____

Goals	Evidence and Comments
1. Growth in understanding social studies concepts	_____ _____ _____
2. Growth in building social studies skills	_____ _____ _____
3. Growth in thinking critically and creatively	_____ _____ _____
4. Growth in developing democratic values and civic responsibility	_____ _____ _____

Summary of Portfolio Assessment

For This Review			Since Last Review		
Excellent	**Good**	**Fair**	**Improving**	**About the Same**	**Not as Good**

Date _____

Dear Family Members,

Here are samples of social studies work that your child and I have chosen for portfolio assessment. Please ask your child to explain what he or she has done. Then write a short note to your child in the space below, telling your thoughts about what you have seen. Please have your child bring the portfolio, with your note, back to school.

Sincerely,

_____

Dear _____

Family Member

_____

Unit 1 Test

Part One: Test Your Understanding (2 points each)

DIRECTIONS: *Match the phrases on the left with the words on the right. Then write the correct letter in the space.*

1. _____ a model of the Earth that is round like a ball

2. _____ the imaginary line halfway between the North Pole and the South Pole

3. _____ a person who lives in a community

4. _____ a group of citizens that makes rules for a community

5. _____ a leader of a city or town government

6. _____ a person who works as a leader in the courts

7. _____ a member of a family who lived a long time ago

8. _____ the way people do something

9. _____ the way of life of a group of people

10. _____ a person who starts a community

A. ancestor

B. equator

C. founder

D. judge

E. mayor

F. government

G. citizen

H. custom

I. culture

J. globe

(continued)

NAME _____ DATE _____

Part Two: Test Your Skills (16 points)

DIRECTIONS: Use the map of Arizona to answer the questions.

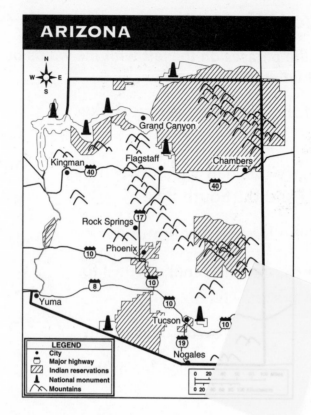

11. What is the direction from Yuma to Tucson? _____

12. What symbol is used to show a mountain? _____

13. How far is it from Flagstaff to Kingman? _____

14. What is the direction from Phoenix to Rock Springs? _____

15. What city is north of Nogales? _____

16. What city is near a national monument? _____

17. What city is south of Kingman? _____

18. How far is it from Flagstaff to Grand Canyon? _____

(continued)

Part Three: Apply What You Have Learned

DIRECTIONS: *Complete each of the following activities.*

19. The Continents (7 points)

Draw a line from each continent map to the name of the continent.

Africa

ntarctica

sia

Australia

Europe

North
America

South
America

(continued)

20. The Compass Rose (8 points)

Write the names of the four points of the compass rose on the correct lines.

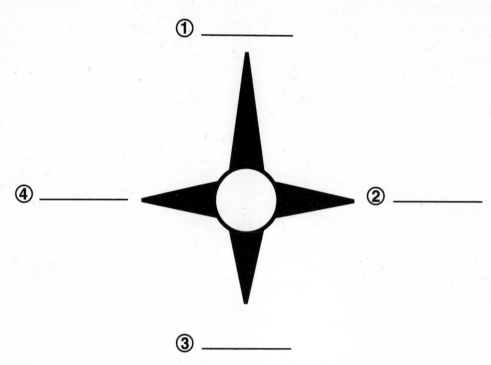

① _____

④ _____

② _____

③ _____

21. Community Resources (9 points)

Draw a circle around the resources you will find in every community.

plants	ocean	soil
bridges	farms	water
airport	people	horses

22. Who Came First? (12 points)

Over the years, four groups of people came to Yuma, Arizona. In what order did these groups come? Place a 1 by the group that came first, a 2 by the group that came second, a 3 by the group that came third, and a 4 by the group that came fourth.

_____ Anglos   _____ Chinese railroad workers

_____ Quechan Indians   _____ Spanish missionaries

(continued)

23. *Making Groups (18 points)*

Each column of words below tells about one big idea. Under the big ideas are words that tell about the ideas. Write each of the words in the box on a line under the big idea where it belongs.

ancestor	custom	government
compass rose	equator	judge

Location	**Community**	**History**
map	citizen	founder
hemisphere	law	culture
_____	_____	_____
_____	_____	_____

24. *In Your Own Words (10 points)*

Your school is a community. One person who is part of the school community is your teacher. You and your classmates are also part of the school community. Write the names or jobs of two other people who are members of your school community.

Individual Performance Task
Make Your Own Map

Draw a map of a place you know. It could be your bedroom, your classroom, a part of the school, the street where you live, or a room in your home. Be sure to include a title, a compass rose, and a map key.

_____

Compass Rose	Map Key

Group Performance Task

Basic Resources

Every community has the same basic resources—soil, water, plants, and people. In this task your group will study the resources of your community and make a poster that shows the resources you think are the most important.

Step 1 Think about your community and about the ways people use resources. Discuss the following questions in your group.

Soil What is the soil like in your community? What color is it? How do people use the soil in your community? What things are found on, in, or under the soil?

Water Do you have rivers, an ocean, lakes, or ponds? How do people use these water resources?

Plants What kinds of plants grow in your community? Are there farmers in your community? If so, what types of crops do the farmers grow?

People What different cultures are there in your community? What ages are the people in your community? What are some of the jobs people have in your community?

Step 2 As a group, make a list of two pictures you could draw for each resource. The pictures should show the most important ways people use the resources in your community. Everyone in the group should agree on these pictures.

Step 3 Each person in the group should draw at least one of the pictures. Be sure to write under each picture what it is.

Step 4 Collect all the pictures. Arrange them on a sheet of posterboard to make a poster. Give your poster a title, and display it in a public place.

Unit 2 Test

Part One: Test Your Understanding (2 points each)

DIRECTIONS: *Match the phrases on the left with the words on the right. Then write the correct letter in the space.*

1. _____ a place where ships can dock

2. _____ a boat that carries people and goods over water

3. _____ a shallow place in a waterway that is easy to cross

4. _____ something found in nature that is useful to people

5. _____ a resource such as oil or coal

6. _____ the place where the leaders of a country meet and work

7. _____ the building where lawmakers meet

A. capital city

B. ford

C. port

D. capitol

E. fuel

F. ferry

G. natural resource

DIRECTIONS: *Circle the letter of the best answer.*

8. Which of these is a physical feature?
- **A.** factory
- **B.** lake
- **C.** boat
- **D.** bridge

9. A place where ships can stay safe from high waves and strong winds is a
- **A.** harbor.
- **B.** coast.
- **C.** ford.
- **D.** gateway.

(continued)

10. A community in which buying and selling goods is
the main work is a
   A. natural resource center.
   B. capital city.
   C. trading center.
   D. county seat.

11. To manufacture something means to
   A. grow it.
   B. open it.
   C. sell it.
   D. make it.

12. Who grows crops?
   A. a mayor
   B. a teacher
   C. a farmer
   D. a trader

13. Which of these is an example of a mineral?
   A. gold
   B. corn
   C. fish
   D. cattle

14. Which of these is a growing season?
   A. the water needed to make crops grow
   B. the soils the crops need
   C. the months when crops can grow
   D. the resources that crops make

(continued)

Part Two: Test Your Skills (20 points)

DIRECTIONS: Use the map of Missouri to answer the questions.

15. What is the state capital of Missouri? _____

16. In what direction is Jefferson City from St. Joseph? _____

17. What city is southeast of Jefferson City? _____

18. What city is north of Jefferson City? _____

19. What state is north of Missouri? _____

(continued)

Part Three: Apply What You Have Learned

DIRECTIONS: Complete each of the following activities.

20. **Understanding the Steps in a Diagram (12 points)**
    Number the pictures to show how wood goes from being part
    of a tree to being part of a house.

___ ___   ___ ___   ___ ___   ___ ___

21. **In Your Own Words (10 points)**
    List five human-made features in your community.

    a. _____

    b. _____

    c. _____

    d. _____

    e. _____

(continued)

22. *Using a Landform Map (12 points)*

Use the landform map of Washington to answer the questions.

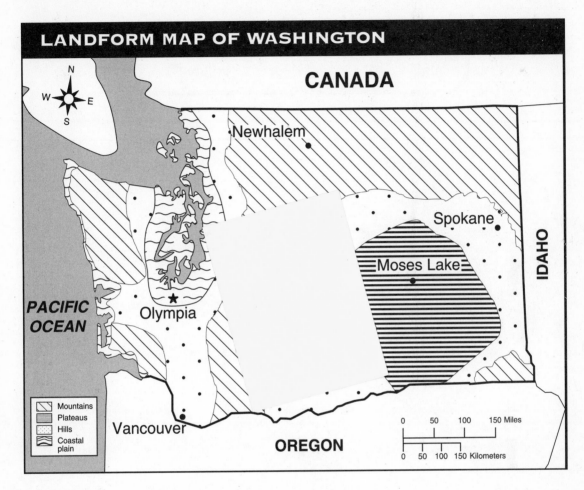

LANDFORM MAP OF WASHINGTON

CANADA

Newhalem

Spokane

Moses Lake

PACIFIC OCEAN

Olympia

IDAHO

Mountains
Plateaus
Hills
Coastal plain

Vancouver

OREGON

0   50   100   150 Miles

0   50   100   150 Kilometers

a. What city is located in the mountains? _____

b. What landform is around the city of Moses Lake?

_____

c. What landform is near the city of Seattle? _____

d. What city is in an area of hills? _____

(continued)

23. *Landforms (18 points)*
    Find each physical feature or body of water on the diagram,
    and write the name in the correct location.

> | | | |
> |---|---|---|
> | mountain range | coast | peninsula |
> | plain | river | valley |

Individual Performance Task

Show the Steps

A set of pictures can help you understand how something works. In this task you are going to draw pictures that show how something is done or how something works.

Step 1: Choose a process that you can show by drawing four pictures. You may choose a process from this list or think of your own process and get your teacher's approval.

- bringing a food product from farm to kitchen
- giving a pet a bath
- the changing of the seasons
- manufacturing something
- following daily school events
- making something, such as cookies

Step 2: Draw your pictures in the boxes. Write sentences under the pictures to explain the process.

1	2	3	4

1. _____

2. _____

3. _____

4. _____

Group Performance Task
Making Maps

Every community is in a county. Every state has many counties. In this task your group will make a wall map of your county.

Step 1: Use library resources to find out the size of your county. Make a list of these things in your county.
- cities
- towns
- county seat
- historical places
- major physical features
- major roads and highways

Step 2: As a group, decide what you are going to put on your wall map. You do not have to put everything about the county on the map. Groups may show different things on their maps.

Step 3: Divide up the tasks for drawing the wall map. Make sure everyone does about the same amount of work.

Step 4: Draw your wall map. Be sure to include a title, a map key, and a compass rose. Display your wall map in a public place when you have finished.

Unit 3 Test

Part One: Test Your Understanding (4 points each)

DIRECTIONS: *Match the phrases on the left with the words on the right. Then write the correct letter in the space provided.*

1. _____ what a person believes about God or a
set of gods

2. _____ a person who comes to live in a country
from another country

3. _____ the chance to have a better way of life

4. _____ books, poetry, stories, and plays

5. _____ culture left to a person by his or her
ancestors

6. _____ a special celebration to remember a
person or event important to the people
of a community

7. _____ customs or ways of doing things that are
passed from parents to children

A. heritage

B. opportunity

C. tradition

D. holiday

E. immigrant

F. literature

G. religion

(continued)

Part Two: Test Your Skills (15 points)

DIRECTIONS: Use the product map of Georgia to answer the
questions on the next page.

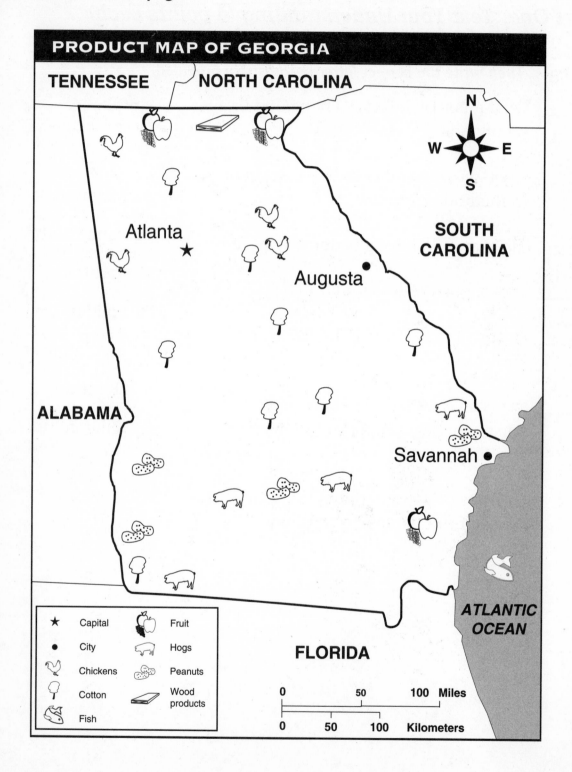

(continued)

8. In how many places in Georgia is cotton grown? _____

9. What product is found only off the southeast coast

of Georgia? _____

10. In what part of Georgia are wood products made?

_____

11. In how many places in Georgia are peanuts grown? _____

12. What animals are raised along the northwestern

border of Georgia? _____

(continued)

Part Three: Apply What You Have Learned

DIRECTIONS: Complete each of the following activities.

13. Reading a Table (15 points)

Use the information in the table to answer the questions that follow.

IMMIGRANTS TO AMERICAN CITIES 1990		
Immigrants from	Houston, TX	Washington, DC
China	473	802
India	854	1,465
Korea	263	1,940
Mexico	34,973	1,056
Vietnam	2,014	2,188

a. Which city had more immigrants from Mexico?

_____

b. Which city had more immigrants from China?

_____

c. What country had the most immigrants going to Washington, DC?

_____

d. What city had more immigrants from Korea?

_____

e. How many immigrants from India went to Washington, DC?

_____

(continued)

14. Reasons for Immigration (16 points)

Give four reasons why people move to a new country.

a. _____

b. _____

c. _____

d. _____

15. Celebrating the New Year (6 points)

Draw a line from the peoples on the left to the way
they celebrate the New Year.

Vietnamese

celebrate *Oshogatsu*
eat *ozoni*, a special soup
clean house

African Americans

celebrate *Kwanzaa*
have a big feast, or *karamu*
light candles

Japanese

celebrate *Tet*
eat *bahn day*, special rice cakes
give children money in small red
envelopes

16. In Your Own Words (10 points)

Tell how you and your family celebrate a holiday.
Include details about the traditions your family
follows for this holiday.

(continued)

17. *The Culture of India (10 points)*

Use the words in the box to complete the sentences below.

Hindi	Islam	sitar
Hinduism	sari	folktale

a. The main language spoken in India is _____.

b. A _____ is a story that teaches an important lesson.

c. The dress worn by many women in India is a _____.

d. Indian musicians play a stringed instrument called a

_____.

e. The two main religions in India are _____ and

_____.

Individual
Performance Task

Table Talk

A table is a way to organize information. It also helps you to compare things easily. In this task you are going to organize information in a table and then answer some questions.

Step 1 Organize these facts about immigration into a table.

Immigration to the United States from 1961 to 1970

    Immigrants from Europe 1,238,600
    Immigrants from Asia 445,300
    Immigrants from South America 228,300
    Immigrants from Africa 39,300

Immigration to the United States from 1981 to 1990

    Immigrants from Europe 593,300
    Immigrants from Asia 2,478,000
    Immigrants from South America 370,100
    Immigrants from Africa 156,400

Step 2 Use the information in your table to answer these questions.

1. What continent had the most immigrants to the

United States from 1961 to 1970? _____

2. What continent had the most immigrants to the

United States from 1981 to 1990? _____

3. What are two patterns you can notice about the

information in the table? _____

_____

_____

Group Performance Task

The Holiday Table

A holiday is a special day for remembering a person or an event that is important to people in a community. People around the world celebrate holidays in different ways. In this task your group will look at holidays around the world, choose one, and then present a talk about this holiday.

Step 1 With the help of your teacher, choose one of these holidays or any other that your teacher suggests.

COUNTRY	HOLIDAY	DATE
Australia-New Zealand	Anzac Day	April 25
Canada	Remembrance Day	November 11
China	Lunar New Year	February
France	Bastille Day	July 14
India	Dewali (Deepavali, Festival of Lights)	November
Iran	New Year (Novruz)	March
Saudi Arabia	Eid al-Fitr	Varies
Spain	Día de los Tres Reyes (Three Kings' Day)	January 6

Step 2 Each student in the group should look for information on the holiday you selected. Use your textbook and library materials to find information about the holiday. Find out what people do on that day.

Step 3 Each group will give a five-minute talk to the class about the holiday. Each group member should tell something about the meaning of the holiday and/or how it is celebrated. Each person should have a picture or drawing that explains some part of the holiday. Then display your pictures where everyone can see them.

Unit 4 Test

Part One: Test Your Understanding (4 points each)

DIRECTIONS: *Match the phrases on the left with the words on the right. Then write the correct letter in the space provided.*

1. _____ something one person does for another

2. _____ out in the countryside, away from cities

3. _____ the wish for a product or service

4. _____ trade between different countries

5. _____ money paid for work

6. _____ person who buys a product or a service

7. _____ resources needed to make a product

8. _____ when different companies make and sell the same product

9. _____ machines, tools, and materials that make doing things easier and faster

10. _____ to send a product or resource of one country to another country

A. consumer

B. service

C. rural

D. technology

E. wage

F. raw materials

G. competition

H. demand

I. export

J. international trade

(continued)

NAME _____ DATE _____

DIRECTIONS: *Circle the letter of the best answer.*

11. What products or services do the Amish buy from other communities?

    A. quilts

    B. a doctor's help

    C. jellies and jams

    D. vegetables

12. What are human resources?

    A. raw materials

    B. money used to make products

    C. people who work for a company

    D. marketing plans

13. The people who make products are

    A. producers.

    B. consumers.

    C. users.

    D. buyers.

14. What is the purpose of an advertisement?

    A. to sell products or services

    B. to entertain people

    C. to teach people what is important

    D. to make people work harder

15. An import is a product that is

    A. made for the first time.

    B. sold to another country.

    C. sold only in markets.

    D. brought into a country from another country.

(continued)

Part Two: Test Your Skills (20 points)

DIRECTIONS: Use the grid map of Pennsylvania to answer the questions.

PENNSYLVANIA			
1	**2**	**3**	**4**

A — Erie

B — Scranton, Williamsport

C — Altoona, Pittsburgh, Allentown

D — Uniontown, Harrisburg ★, Lancaster, Philadelphia

16. In which square is Philadelphia located? _____

17. What city is in square A–1? _____

18. In which square is Williamsport located? _____

19. What city is in square C–2? _____

20. In which square is the state capital located? _____

(continued)

Part Three: Apply What You Have Learned

DIRECTIONS: *Complete each of the following activities.*

21. *In Your Own Words (10 points)*

Choose one of these pairs of words. Tell why they go together and what they mean.

> Supply and Demand
>
> Export and Import

22. *Products and Services (10 points)*

List three products that you use every day.

a. _____

b. _____

c. _____

List three services you can find in your community.

d. _____

e. _____

f. _____

(continued)

List three products that come from a rural place.

g. _____

h. _____

i. _____

Give one example of competition between
businesses in your community.

j. _____

_____

_____

Individual
Performance Task
Picture Something You Like

Imagine that your class has decided to take a survey to
see what things students like. You will need to interview
other students. Then you will make a pictograph. A
pictograph has small pictures of objects that show how
many things are in a group. Your pictograph should
show other students what you found out. Follow the
steps below.

Step 1 Decide what you will use for the topic of your
pictograph. Some ideas are favorite ice-cream
flavors, favorite cafeteria foods, or favorite
sports teams.

Step 2 Make a list of four or five choices for your subject.
Draw small pictures to stand for these choices.
You might use different-colored ice-cream cones,
different foods, or different team symbols.

Step 3 Then ask people, "Which of these is your
favorite?" Be sure to keep a correct count of the
number of people you ask and their answers.
Ask at least five people your question.

Step 4 Make your pictograph. A pictograph has
three parts:
- a title to explain what it is about
- pictures for the choices
- a key to explain what the pictures stand for

Step 5 Ask a classmate to check your pictograph to see if
anything is missing.

Step 6 Display your pictograph where others can see it.

Group Performance Task

Trading Places

International trade is trade between countries. Some products that are bought and sold in international trade are clothing, foods, and cars. In this task your group will make an International Trade Poster. The poster will show some things each student has that are part of international trade.

Step 1 Each group member should look at home for five products that were made in other countries and then sold in the United States. The products might be clothing, food products, electrical goods, sports equipment, or cars. List these products along with the country where they came from.

Step 2 Now draw products made in other countries on sheets of 6" x 6" white paper. Each paper should have a picture of a product, a label under the picture, and the name of the student.

Step 3 Paste an outline map of the world (8½"x 11") in the center of a poster board or a piece of mural-size art paper. Now paste your pictures around the world map, and then draw a line from each product to the place on the map from which it came. Be neat when you make your lines because many will be going to the same place.

Step 4 Label the poster *International Trade.* Display the poster where others can see it.

Unit 5 Test

Part One: Test Your Understanding (3 points each)

DIRECTIONS: *Match the phrases on the left with the words on the right. Then write the correct letter in the space provided.*

1. ____ money paid to a government to run a city

2. ____ a set of rules the Pilgrims agreed to follow

3. ____ leader of a state government

4. ____ a group of citizens who make decisions in a court

5. ____ respect for the flag and what it stands for

6. ____ love of your country

7. ____ a song about the love of your country

8. ____ the person who wrote "The Star-Spangled Banner"

9. ____ the first elected black African president to lead the government of South Africa

A. Francis Scott Key

B. allegiance

C. Mayflower Compact

D. taxes

E. governor

F. jury

G. patriotism

H. anthem

I. Nelson Mandela

DIRECTIONS: *Circle the letter of the best answer.*

10. The group of people who are elected to solve problems for a town or city is the
    A. court.
    B. Congress.
    C. council.
    D. community.

(continued)

11. What did Hiawatha use to tell others of the Iroquois laws?

    A. posters

    B. signs

    C. books

    D. wampum belts

12. What does the Constitution describe?

    A. how states can build highways and bridges

    B. how the United States government works

    C. how the city government provides services

    D. how people show their patriotism

13. Why does each state need its own government?

    A. Each state has its own problems to solve.

    B. Some states have more people than other states.

    C. States need to get taxes from the people.

    D. All states need a state anthem.

14. Why are there 50 stars on the United States flag?

    A. The stars stand for the Presidents of the United States.

    B. One star is added to the flag every ten years.

    C. The stars are for the heroes of the country.

    D. There is one star for each state.

(continued)

Part Two: Test Your Skills (16 points)

DIRECTIONS: Use the information on the map to answer the questions.

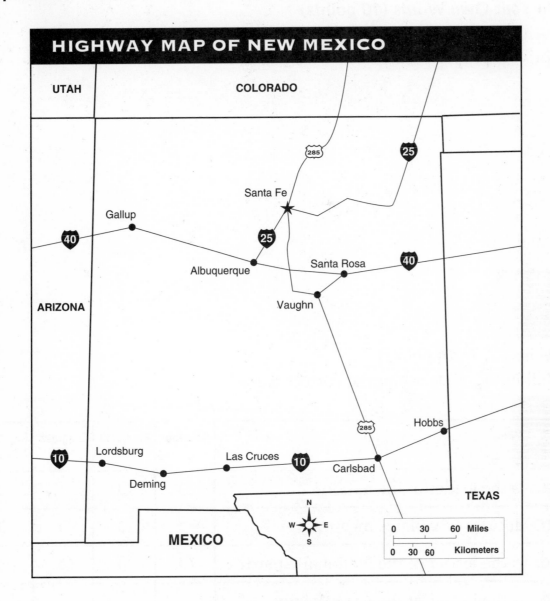

15. How many miles is it from Albuquerque to Gallup? _____

16. How many kilometers is it from Deming to Lordsburg? _____

17. Santa Rosa is how many miles from Vaughn? _____

18. Carlsbad is how many kilometers from Albuquerque? _____

(continued)

Part Three: Apply What You Have Learned

DIRECTIONS: *Complete each of the following activities.*

19. In Your Own Words (10 points)

What is the difference between public property and private property? Give one example of each.

20. Who . . . ? (14 points)

Fill in the circle under the correct name.

Who . . .	Governor	President	Congress	Supreme Court
a. is the leader of the nation?	O	O	O	O
b. decides what laws mean?	O	O	O	O
c. is the leader of the National Guard?	O	O	O	O
d. is the leader of the Army, Navy, Air Force, and Marines?	O	O	O	O
e. makes new laws?	O	O	O	O
f. signs treaties with other nations?	O	O	O	O
g. are the senators and representatives?	O	O	O	O

(continued)

21. *Services (18 points)*

Governments provide services to the people. In the chart below, list two services provided by local, state, and national governments.

GOVERNMENT SERVICES		
Services Provided by Local Governments	Services Provided by State Governments	Services Provided by National Government

Individual
Performance Task
It's Official

There are many government officials at the three levels of government in the United States—national, state, and local. In this task you are going to find out who these officials are and then make a chart that shows their positions and names.

Step 1 Use library resources or ask your teacher or another adult to find out the names of the men and women who hold these government offices. Your teacher may add other jobs that are special to your area.

National Level	**State Level**
President of the United States	Governor
Vice President of the United States	Lieutenant Governor
Member of Congress in the House of Representatives	Representatives in the state legislature
Senators in the Senate	**Local Level**
Chief Justice of the United States Supreme Court	Mayor
	Member of local council

Step 2 Make a chart showing each of these groups of officials. Label your chart to show the level of government. You may also want to look in newspapers and magazines to find pictures of the officials and paste them on your chart.

Step 3 Display your chart in a place where others can see it.

Group Performance Task
Election Day

The governor of your state has an important position. In this task you are going to have a mock election for governor. A mock election is a pretend election.

Step 1 The class should divide into two groups. Each group will select one person to be the candidate for governor of your state.

Step 2 As a group, decide what you want the candidate for governor to do when elected. Make a list of three or four things the candidate will promise to do.

Step 3 Some people in the group should make campaign posters that tell why people should vote for their candidate. Other members of the group should make handouts to give to people explaining why they should vote for your candidate. The candidate should prepare a speech of two or three minutes to tell why he or she should be elected.

Step 4 Hold an assembly for other classes in your school. Display the posters and give the students who attend the assembly the handouts. Then have each candidate make a speech. At the end of the assembly, have all the students vote to elect the governor.

Unit 6 Test

Part One: Test Your Understanding (5 points each)

DIRECTIONS: *Match the phrases on the left with the words on the right. Then write the correct letter in the space provided.*

1. _____ a place to store water

2. _____ ten years

3. _____ one hundred years

4. _____ a place where people no longer live

5. _____ the capital city of the Aztecs

6. _____ waterways built by people

7. _____ wide roads over water

8. _____ the land and peoples under the control of a powerful nation

9. _____ the largest city in the world

10. _____ anything that makes air, land, or water unclean

A. canals

B. ghost town

C. pollution

D. reservoir

E. Mexico City

F. century

G. empire

H. Tenochtitlán

I. decade

J. causeways

(continued)

NAME _____ DATE _____

Part Two: *Test Your Skills (25 points)*

DIRECTIONS: **Use the maps to answer the questions.**

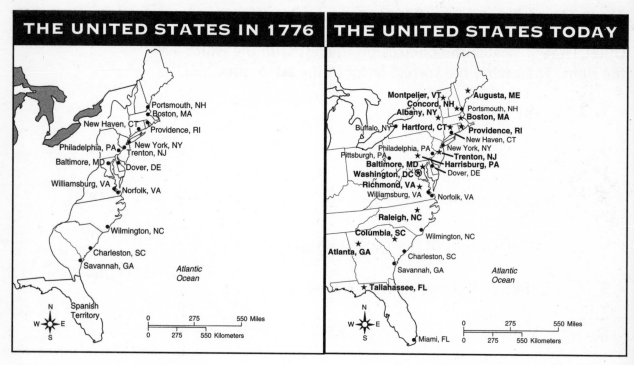

Map 1   **Map 2**

11. What states are on Map 2 but not on Map 1? _____

_____

12. What cities in Pennsylvania are on Map 2 but not on

Map 1? _____

13. What city in Georgia is on Map 2 but not on Map 1? _____

14. Where was the nation's capital city in 1776? _____

_____

15. Where is the nation's capital city today? _____

(continued)

Part Three: Apply What You Have Learned

DIRECTIONS: *Complete each of the following activities.*

16. *Short Answers (15 points)*
Answer the following questions.

a. List three types of disasters that can cause a place
to change.

_____

_____

_____

b. List three types of technology people use today
that most people did not have 100 years ago.

_____

_____

_____

c. List three ways people in Mexico City can help
lower the amount of air pollution in their city.

_____

_____

_____

(continued)

17. *In Your Own Words (10 points)*

Your teacher has asked you to write a history of your community. Tell in your own words the people you would talk to and the places you would go to get information for your report. Explain why you chose those people and places.

Individual Performance Task

Change Over Time

Towns and communities change over time. In this task
you are going to make three bar graphs that show the
changes in the number of people who live in three
different places. After making your graphs, you will
use the information to make conclusions.

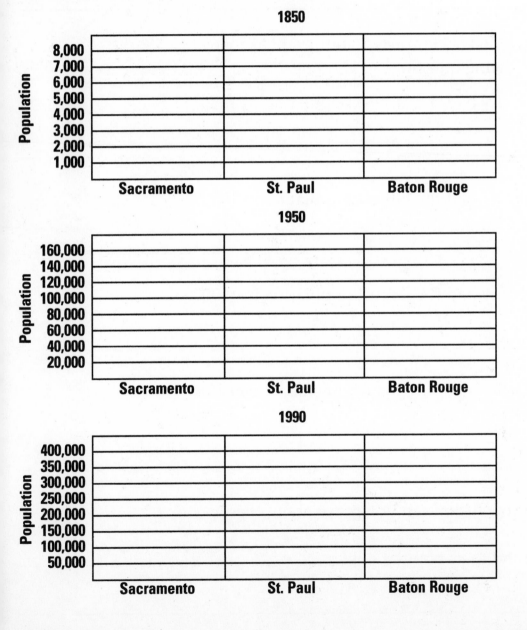

(continued)

Step 1 Use the information in the table below to make three different population graphs on the grids on page 59.

	SACRAMENTO, CA	ST. PAUL, MN	BATON ROUGE, LA
Year	Population	Population	Population
1850	6,820	1,112	3,905
1950	137,572	311,349	125,629
1990	369,365	272,235	219,531

Step 2 After you have completed your graphs, answer the following questions.

Which city had the largest population in 1850?

_____

Which city had the largest population in 1950?

_____

Which city had the largest population in 1990?

_____

Which city's population declined between 1950 and 1990?

_____

What conclusion can you make about these

cities and their populations? _____

_____

Group Performance Task
Then and Now

Places change over time. In this task your group is going to make two maps. One will show an area of your community or an area near your school as it was ten years ago. The other map will show the same area as it is today.

Step 1 With your teacher's help, decide the area your map will show. It may be a part of your community, town, or city or the area around the school.

Step 2 Make a list of people you can talk to who will know about the area your map shows. This list can include school officials (principal, teachers, staff, custodians, bus drivers), parents and grandparents, community officials, and other citizens in the community. You may also want to visit your school library, public library, and the local historical society.

Step 3 Make a rough sketch of the area you have chosen as it looks today. Each member of the group should show this map to the people on your list and ask them how this area looked ten years ago. Write down their answers.

Step 4 Make a rough sketch of the area as it looked ten years ago. Go back to the people you talked with, and ask them whether the map is what they remember. The map may help them remember more information.

Step 5 Make two final poster-sized maps. On the map titles, include the dates they represent. Use labels to show the areas that have changed in the past ten years. Display your maps in a place where others can see them.

Answer Key

ANSWERS

Unit 1 Test

Part One: Test Your Understanding (2 points each)

DIRECTIONS: Match the phrases on the left with the words on the right. Then write the correct letter in the space.

1. **J** a model of the Earth that is round like a ball

2. **B** the imaginary line halfway between the North Pole and the South Pole

3. **G** a person who lives in a community

4. **F** a group of citizens that makes rules for a community

5. **E** a leader of a city or town government

6. **D** a person who works as a leader in the courts

7. **A** a member of a family who lived a long time ago

8. **H** the way people do something

9. **I** the way of life of a group of people

10. **C** a person who starts a community

A. ancestor

B. equator

C. founder

D. judge

E. mayor

F. government

G. citizen

H. custom

I. culture

J. globe

(continued)

UNIT 1 TEST   Assessment Program 15

Part Two: Test Your Skills (16 points)

DIRECTIONS: Use the map of Arizona to answer the questions.

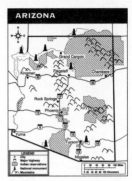

11. What is the direction from Yuma to Tucson? **east**

12. What symbol is used to show a mountain? **a mountain shape**

13. How far is it from Flagstaff to Kingman? **about 140 miles**

14. What is the direction from Phoenix to Rock Springs? **north**

15. What city is north of Nogales? **Tucson**

16. What city is near a national monument? **Tucson or Flagstaff**

17. What city is south of Kingman? **Yuma**

18. How far is it from Flagstaff to Grand Canyon? **about 80 miles**

(continued)

16   Assessment Program   UNIT 1 TEST

Part Three: Apply What You Have Learned

DIRECTIONS: Complete each of the following activities.

19. The Continents (7 points)

Draw a line from each continent map to the name of the continent.

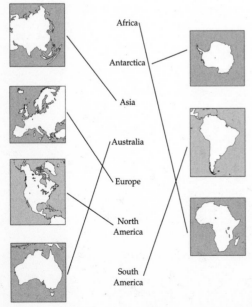

Africa

Antarctica

Asia

Australia

Europe

North America

South America

(continued)

UNIT 1 TEST   Assessment Program 17

20. The Compass Rose (8 points)

Write the names of the four points of the compass rose on the correct lines.

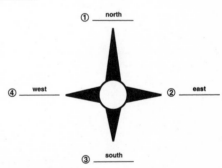

① north

④ west   ② east

③ south

21. Community Resources (9 points)

Draw a circle around the resources you will find in every community.

(plants)   ocean   (soil)

bridges   farms   (water)

airport   (people)   horses

22. Who Came First? (12 points)

Over the years, four groups of people came to Yuma, Arizona. In what order did these groups come? Place a 1 by the group that came first, a 2 by the group that came second, a 3 by the group that came third, and a 4 by the group that came fourth.

3 Anglos   **4** Chinese railroad workers

1 Quechan Indians   **2** Spanish missionaries

(continued)

18   Assessment Program   UNIT 1 TEST

ANSWERS

23. *Making Groups (18 points)*

Each column of words below tells about one big idea. Under the big ideas are words that tell about the ideas. Write each of the words in the box on a line under the big idea where it belongs.

ancestor	custom	government
compass rose	equator	judge

Location	**Community**	**History**
map	citizen	founder
hemisphere	law	culture
compass rose	**judge**	**ancestor**
equator	**government**	**custom**

24. *In Your Own Words (10 points)*

Your school is a community. One person who is part of the school community is your teacher. You and your classmates are also part of the school community. Write the names or jobs of two other people who are members of your school community.

Possible responses: Students may name individuals or they may identify them by the jobs they do. For example, aide, bus driver, cafeteria worker, custodian, nurse, principal, and secretary.

Individual Performance Task
Make Your Own Map

Draw a map of a place you know. It could be your bedroom, your classroom, a part of the school, the street where you live, or a room in your home. Be sure to include a title, a compass rose, and a map key.

Compass Rose	Map Key

Group Performance Task
Basic Resources

Every community has the same basic resources—soil, water, plants, and people. In this task your group will study the resources of your community and make a poster that shows the resources you think are the most important.

Step 1 Think about your community and about the ways people use resources. Discuss the following questions in your group.

Soil What is the soil like in your community? What color is it? How do people use the soil in your community? What things are found on, in, or under the soil?

Water Do you have rivers, an ocean, lakes, or ponds? How do people use these water resources?

Plants What kinds of plants grow in your community? Are there farmers in your community? If so, what types of crops do the farmers grow?

People What different cultures are there in your community? What ages are the people in your community? What are some of the jobs people have in your community?

Step 2 As a group, make a list of two pictures you could draw for each resource. The pictures should show the most important ways people use the resources in your community. Everyone in the group should agree on these pictures.

Step 3 Each person in the group should draw at least one of the pictures. Be sure to write under each picture what it is.

Step 4 Collect all the pictures. Arrange them on a sheet of posterboard to make a poster. Give your poster a title, and display it in a public place.

ANSWERS

Unit 2 Test

Part One: Test Your Understanding (2 points each)

DIRECTIONS: *Match the phrases on the left with the words on the right. Then write the correct letter in the space.*

1. __C__ a place where ships can dock

2. __F__ a boat that carries people and goods over water

3. __B__ a shallow place in a waterway that is easy to cross

4. __G__ something found in nature that is useful to people

5. __E__ a resource such as oil or coal

6. __A__ the place where the leaders of a country meet and work

7. __D__ the building where lawmakers meet

A. capital city
B. ford
C. port
D. capitol
E. fuel
F. ferry
G. natural resource

DIRECTIONS: *Circle the letter of the best answer.*

8. Which of these is a physical feature?
   A. factory
   (B.) lake
   C. boat
   D. bridge

9. A place where ships can stay safe from high waves and strong winds is a
   (A.) harbor.
   B. coast.
   C. ford.
   D. gateway.

10. A community in which buying and selling goods is the main work is a
    A. natural resource center.
    B. capital city.
    (C.) trading center.
    D. county seat.

11. To manufacture something means to
    A. grow it.
    B. open it.
    C. sell it.
    (D.) make it.

12. Who grows crops?
    A. a mayor
    B. a teacher
    (C.) a farmer
    D. a trader

13. Which of these is an example of a mineral?
    (A.) gold
    B. corn
    C. fish
    D. cattle

14. Which of these is a growing season?
    A. the water needed to make crops grow
    B. the soils the crops need
    (C.) the months when crops can grow
    D. the resources that crops make

(continued)

Assessment Program 23

24 Assessment Program

(continued)

Part Two: Test Your Skills (20 points)

DIRECTIONS: *Use the map of Missouri to answer the questions.*

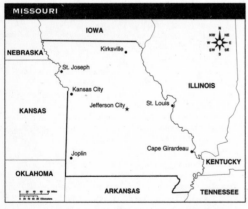

15. What is the state capital of Missouri? __Jefferson City__

16. In what direction is Jefferson City from St. Joseph? __southeast__

17. What city is southeast of Jefferson City? __Cape Girardeau__

18. What city is north of Jefferson City? __Kirksville__

19. What state is north of Missouri? __Iowa__

(continued)

Assessment Program 25

Part Three: Apply What You Have Learned

DIRECTIONS: *Complete each of the following activities.*

20. **Understanding the Steps in a Diagram (12 points)**
    Number the pictures to show how wood goes from being part of a tree to being part of a house.

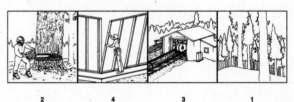

    2   4   3   1

21. *In Your Own Words (10 points)*
    List five human-made features in your community.

    a. __Possible responses: Any feature made by humans is correct.__

    b. _____

    c. _____

    d. _____

    e. _____

(continued)

26 Assessment Program

ANSWERS

22. *Using a Landform Map (12 points)*

Use the landform map of Washington to answer the questions.

a. What city is located in the mountains? <u>Newhalem</u>

b. What landform is around the city of Moses Lake?

<u>a plateau</u>

c. What landform is near the city of Seattle? <u>a plain</u>

d. What city is in an area of hills? <u>Spokane or Vancouver</u>

(continued)

23. *Landforms (18 points)*

Find each physical feature or body of water on the diagram, and write the name in the correct location.

| mountain range | coast | peninsula |
| plain | river | valley |

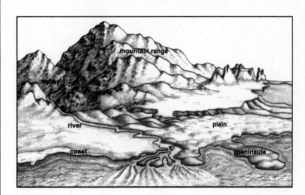

Individual Performance Task
Show the Steps

A set of pictures can help you understand how something works. In this task you are going to draw pictures that show how something is done or how something works.

Step 1: Choose a process that you can show by drawing four pictures. You may choose a process from this list or think of your own process and get your teacher's approval.
- bringing a food product from farm to kitchen
- giving a pet a bath
- the changing of the seasons
- manufacturing something
- following daily school events
- making something, such as cookies

Step 2: Draw your pictures in the boxes. Write sentences under the pictures to explain the process.

1	2	3	4

1. _____

2. _____

3. _____

4. _____

Group Performance Task
Making Maps

Every community is in a county. Every state has many counties. In this task your group will make a wall map of your county.

Step 1: Use library resources to find out the size of your county. Make a list of these things in your county.
- cities
- towns
- county seat
- historical places
- major physical features
- major roads and highways

Step 2: As a group, decide what you are going to put on your wall map. You do not have to put everything about the county on the map. Groups may show different things on their maps.

Step 3: Divide up the tasks for drawing the wall map. Make sure everyone does about the same amount of work.

Step 4: Draw your wall map. Be sure to include a title, a map key, and a compass rose. Display your wall map in a public place when you have finished.

ANSWERS

Unit 3 Test

Part One: Test Your Understanding (4 points each)

DIRECTIONS: *Match the phrases on the left with the words on the right. Then write the correct letter in the space provided.*

1. __G__ what a person believes about God or a set of gods

2. __E__ a person who comes to live in a country from another country

3. __B__ the chance to have a better way of life

4. __F__ books, poetry, stories, and plays

5. __A__ culture left to a person by his or her ancestors

6. __D__ a special celebration to remember a person or event important to the people of a community

7. __C__ customs or ways of doing things that are passed from parents to children

A. heritage

B. opportunity

C. tradition

D. holiday

E. immigrant

F. literature

G. religion

(continued)

Part Two: Test Your Skills (15 points)

DIRECTIONS: *Use the product map of Georgia to answer the questions on the next page.*

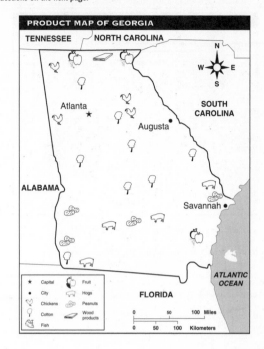

PRODUCT MAP OF GEORGIA

(continued)

8. In how many places in Georgia is cotton grown? __eight__

9. What product is found only off the southeast coast of Georgia? __fish__

10. In what part of Georgia are wood products made? __in the northern part__

11. In how many places in Georgia are peanuts grown? __four__

12. What animals are raised along the northwestern border of Georgia? __chickens__

(continued)

Part Three: Apply What You Have Learned

DIRECTIONS: *Complete each of the following activities.*

13. **Reading a Table (15 points)**
    Use the information in the table to answer the questions that follow.

IMMIGRANTS TO AMERICAN CITIES 1990		
Immigrants from	Houston, TX	Washington, DC
China	473	802
India	854	1,465
Korea	263	1,940
Mexico	34,973	1,056
Vietnam	2,014	2,188

a. Which city had more immigrants from Mexico?

   __Houston__

b. Which city had more immigrants from China?

   __Washington, DC__

c. What country had the most immigrants going to Washington, DC?

   __Vietnam__

d. What city had more immigrants from Korea?

   __Washington, DC__

e. How many immigrants from India went to Washington, DC?

   __1,465__

(continued)

ANSWERS

14. Reasons for Immigration (16 points)

Give four reasons why people move to a new country.

a. Possible responses: adventure, jobs, educational

b. opportunity, better way of life, freedom to practice

c. religion, escape from war, more food

d. _____

15. Celebrating the New Year (6 points)

Draw a line from the peoples on the left to the way they celebrate the New Year.

Vietnamese

celebrate *Oshogatsu*
eat *ozoni*, a special soup
clean house

African Americans

celebrate *Kwanzaa*
have a big feast, or *karamu*
light candles

Japanese

celebrate *Tet*
eat *bahn day*, special rice cakes
give children money in small red envelopes

16. In Your Own Words (10 points)

Tell how you and your family celebrate a holiday. Include details about the traditions your family follows for this holiday.

Accept all reasonable responses.

(continued)

---

17. The Culture of India (10 points)

Use the words in the box to complete the sentences below.

Hindi	Islam	sitar
Hinduism	sari	folktale

a. The main language spoken in India is _____ Hindi _____.

b. A _____ folktale _____ is a story that teaches an important lesson.

c. The dress worn by many women in India is a _____ sari _____.

d. Indian musicians play a stringed instrument called a

_____ sitar _____.

e. The two main religions in India are _____ Hinduism _____ and

_____ Islam _____.

Individual Performance Task
Table Talk

A table is a way to organize information. It also helps you to compare things easily. In this task you are going to organize information in a table and then answer some questions.

Step 1 Organize these facts about immigration into a table.

Immigration to the United States from 1961 to 1970

Immigrants from Europe 1,238,600
Immigrants from Asia 445,300
Immigrants from South America 228,300
Immigrants from Africa 39,300

Immigration to the United States from 1981 to 1990

Immigrants from Europe 593,300
Immigrants from Asia 2,478,000
Immigrants from South America 370,100
Immigrants from Africa 156,400

Step 2 Use the information in your table to answer these questions.

1. What continent had the most immigrants to the

United States from 1961 to 1970? _____ Europe _____

2. What continent had the most immigrants to the

United States from 1981 to 1990? _____ Asia _____

3. What are two patterns you can notice about the

information in the table? Possible responses: More Asians came

to America from 1981 to 1990 than from 1961 to 1970. Fewer Europeans

came to America from 1981 to 1990 than from 1961 to 1970.

Group Performance Task
The Holiday Table

A holiday is a special day for remembering a person or an event that is important to people in a community. People around the world celebrate holidays in different ways. In this task your group will look at holidays around the world, choose one, and then present a talk about this holiday.

Step 1 With the help of your teacher, choose one of these holidays or any other that your teacher suggests.

COUNTRY	HOLIDAY	DATE
Australia-New Zealand	Anzac Day	April 25
Canada	Remembrance Day	November 11
China	Lunar New Year	February
France	Bastille Day	July 14
India	Dewali (Deepavali, Festival of Lights)	November
Iran	New Year (Novruz)	March
Saudi Arabia	Eid al-Fitr	Varies
Spain	Día de los Tres Reyes (Three Kings' Day)	January 6

Step 2 Each student in the group should look for information on the holiday you selected. Use your textbook and library materials to find information about the holiday. Find out what people do on that day.

Step 3 Each group will give a five-minute talk to the class about the holiday. Each group member should tell something about the meaning of the holiday and/or how it is celebrated. Each person should have a picture or drawing that explains some part of the holiday. Then display your pictures where everyone can see them.

ANSWERS

Unit 4 Test

Part One: Test Your Understanding (4 points each)

DIRECTIONS: Match the phrases on the left with the words on the right. Then write the correct letter in the space provided.

1. __B__ something one person does for another

2. __C__ out in the countryside, away from cities

3. __H__ the wish for a product or service

4. __J__ trade between different countries

5. __E__ money paid for work

6. __A__ person who buys a product or a service

7. __F__ resources needed to make a product

8. __G__ when different companies make and sell the same product

9. __D__ machines, tools, and materials that make doing things easier and faster

10. __I__ to send a product or resource of one country to another country

A. consumer

B. service

C. rural

D. technology

E. wage

F. raw materials

G. competition

H. demand

I. export

J. international trade

DIRECTIONS: Circle the letter of the best answer.

11. What products or services do the Amish buy from other communities?
    A. quilts
    B. a doctor's help
    C. jellies and jams
    D. vegetables

12. What are human resources?
    A. raw materials
    B. money used to make products
    C. people who work for a company
    D. marketing plans

13. The people who make products are
    A. producers.
    B. consumers.
    C. users.
    D. buyers.

14. What is the purpose of an advertisement?
    A. to sell products or services
    B. to entertain people
    C. to teach people what is important
    D. to make people work harder

15. An import is a product that is
    A. made for the first time.
    B. sold to another country.
    C. sold only in markets.
    D. brought into a country from another country.

(continued)

Part Two: Test Your Skills (20 points)

DIRECTIONS: Use the grid map of Pennsylvania to answer the questions.

PENNSYLVANIA

	1	2	3	4
A	Erie			
B			Williamsport	Scranton
C	Pittsburgh	Altoona		Allentown
D	Uniontown		Harrisburg / Lancaster	Philadelphia

16. In which square is Philadelphia located? __D–4__

17. What city is in square A–1? __Erie__

18. In which square is Williamsport located? __B–3__

19. What city is in square C–2? __Altoona__

20. In which square is the state capital located? __D–3__

(continued)

Part Three: Apply What You Have Learned

DIRECTIONS: Complete each of the following activities.

21. **In Your Own Words (10 points)**
    Choose one of these pairs of words. Tell why they go together and what they mean.

    > Supply and Demand
    >
    > Export and Import

    Possible responses:
    Supply and Demand — They are both about products and services. Supply is the amount of products or services that is ready for sale. Demand is the amount of products or services people want to buy.
    Export and Import — They are both about trade. An export is a product that is sent out of a country. An import is a product that is brought into a country.

22. **Products and Services (10 points)**
    List three products that you use every day.

    a. __Possible responses: food products, clothing, cars__

    b. _____

    c. _____

    List three services you can find in your community.

    d. __Possible responses: services of a doctor, nurse, teacher, hair stylist, server__

    e. _____

    f. _____

(continued)

70   Assessment Program   ANSWER KEY

ANSWERS

List three products that come from a rural place.

g. **Possible responses: milk, corn, meat, apples**

h. _____

i. _____

Give one example of competition between businesses in your community.

j. **Possible response: different fast food restaurants, clothing stores,**

or automobile dealers that sell the same kinds of products

_____

Individual Performance Task
Picture Something You Like

Imagine that your class has decided to take a survey to see what things students like. You will need to interview other students. Then you will make a pictograph. A pictograph has small pictures of objects that show how many things are in a group. Your pictograph should show other students what you found out. Follow the steps below.

Step 1 Decide what you will use for the topic of your pictograph. Some ideas are favorite ice-cream flavors, favorite cafeteria foods, or favorite sports teams.

Step 2 Make a list of four or five choices for your subject. Draw small pictures to stand for these choices. You might use different-colored ice-cream cones, different foods, or different team symbols.

Step 3 Then ask people, "Which of these is your favorite?" Be sure to keep a correct count of the number of people you ask and their answers. Ask at least five people your question.

Step 4 Make your pictograph. A pictograph has three parts:
- a title to explain what it is about
- pictures for the choices
- a key to explain what the pictures stand for

Step 5 Ask a classmate to check your pictograph to see if anything is missing.

Step 6 Display your pictograph where others can see it.

Group Performance Task
Trading Places

International trade is trade between countries. Some products that are bought and sold in international trade are clothing, foods, and cars. In this task your group will make an International Trade Poster. The poster will show some things each student has that are part of international trade.

Step 1 Each group member should look at home for five products that were made in other countries and then sold in the United States. The products might be clothing, food products, electrical goods, sports equipment, or cars. List these products along with the country where they came from.

Step 2 Now draw products made in other countries on sheets of 6" x 6" white paper. Each paper should have a picture of a product, a label under the picture, and the name of the student.

Step 3 Paste an outline map of the world (8½"x 11") in the center of a poster board or a piece of mural-size art paper. Now paste your pictures around the world map, and then draw a line from each product to the place on the map from which it came. Be neat when you make your lines because many will be going to the same place.

Step 4 Label the poster *International Trade*. Display the poster where others can see it.

ANSWERS

Unit 5 Test

Part One: Test Your Understanding (3 points each)

DIRECTIONS: *Match the phrases on the left with the words on the right. Then write the correct letter in the space provided.*

1. __D__ money paid to a government to run a city

2. __C__ a set of rules the Pilgrims agreed to follow

3. __E__ leader of a state government

4. __F__ a group of citizens who make decisions in a court

5. __B__ respect for the flag and what it stands for

6. __G__ love of your country

7. __H__ a song about the love of your country

8. __A__ the person who wrote "The Star-Spangled Banner"

9. __I__ the first elected black African president to lead the government of South Africa

A. Francis Scott Key

B. allegiance

C. Mayflower Compact

D. taxes

E. governor

F. jury

G. patriotism

H. anthem

I. Nelson Mandela

DIRECTIONS: *Circle the letter of the best answer.*

10. The group of people who are elected to solve problems for a town or city is the
    A. court.
    B. Congress.
    (C.) council.
    D. community.

11. What did Hiawatha use to tell others of the Iroquois laws?
    A. posters
    B. signs
    C. books
    (D.) wampum belts

12. What does the Constitution describe?
    A. how states can build highways and bridges
    (B.) how the United States government works
    C. how the city government provides services
    D. how people show their patriotism

13. Why does each state need its own government?
    (A.) Each state has its own problems to solve.
    B. Some states have more people than other states.
    C. States need to get taxes from the people.
    D. All states need a state anthem.

14. Why are there 50 stars on the United States flag?
    A. The stars stand for the Presidents of the United States.
    B. One star is added to the flag every ten years.
    C. The stars are for the heroes of the country.
    (D.) There is one star for each state.

Part Two: Test Your Skills (16 points)

DIRECTIONS: *Use the information on the map to answer the questions.*

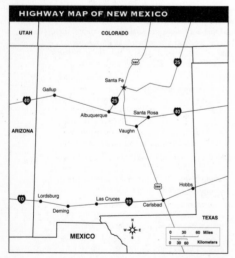

HIGHWAY MAP OF NEW MEXICO

15. How many miles is it from Albuquerque to Gallup? __120 miles__

16. How many kilometers is it from Deming to Lordsburg? __97 kilometers__

17. Santa Rosa is how many miles from Vaughn? __30 miles__

18. Carlsbad is how many kilometers from Albuquerque? __385 kilometers__

Part Three: Apply What You Have Learned

DIRECTIONS: *Complete each of the following activities.*

19. **In Your Own Words (10 points)**
    What is the difference between public property and private property? Give one example of each.
    Possible response:
    Public property belongs to all the people. An example could be city hall, a park, or a library. Private property belongs to one person or a group of people. An example could be a house, a grocery store, or a shopping mall.

20. **Who . . . ? (14 points)**
    Fill in the circle under the correct name.

Who...	Governor	President	Congress	Supreme Court
a. is the leader of the nation?	○	●	○	○
b. decides what laws mean?	○	○	○	●
c. is the leader of the National Guard?	●	○	○	○
d. is the leader of the Army, Navy, Air Force, and Marines?	○	●	○	○
e. makes new laws?	○	○	●	○
f. signs treaties with other nations?	○	●	○	○
g. are the senators and representatives?	○	○	●	○

21. *Services (18 points)*

Governments provide services to the people. In the chart below, list two services provided by local, state, and national governments.

GOVERNMENT SERVICES		
Services Provided by Local Governments	Services Provided by State Governments	Services Provided by National Government
Possible responses: garbage collection, libraries, schools, police and fire protection	Possible responses: driver's licenses, highways, parks, colleges	Possible responses: printing money, military forces, communications with other countries

---

Individual
Performance Task
It's Official

There are many government officials at the three levels of government in the United States—national, state, and local. In this task you are going to find out who these officials are and then make a chart that shows their positions and names.

Step 1 Use library resources or ask your teacher or another adult to find out the names of the men and women who hold these government offices. Your teacher may add other jobs that are special to your area.

National Level	State Level
President of the United States	Governor
Vice President of the United States	Lieutenant Governor
Member of Congress in the House of Representatives	Representatives in the state legislature
Senators in the Senate	**Local Level**
Chief Justice of the United States Supreme Court	Mayor
	Member of local council

Step 2 Make a chart showing each of these groups of officials. Label your chart to show the level of government. You may also want to look in newspapers and magazines to find pictures of the officials and paste them on your chart.

Step 3 Display your chart in a place where others can see it.

Group
Performance Task
Election Day

The governor of your state has an important position. In this task you are going to have a mock election for governor. A mock election is a pretend election.

Step 1 The class should divide into two groups. Each group will select one person to be the candidate for governor of your state.

Step 2 As a group, decide what you want the candidate for governor to do when elected. Make a list of three or four things the candidate will promise to do.

Step 3 Some people in the group should make campaign posters that tell why people should vote for their candidate. Other members of the group should make handouts to give to people explaining why they should vote for your candidate. The candidate should prepare a speech of two or three minutes to tell why he or she should be elected.

Step 4 Hold an assembly for other classes in your school. Display the posters and give the students who attend the assembly the handouts. Then have each candidate make a speech. At the end of the assembly, have all the students vote to elect the governor.

ANSWERS

Unit 6 Test

Part One: Test Your Understanding (5 points each)

DIRECTIONS: Match the phrases on the left with the words on the right. Then write the correct letter in the space provided.

1. __D__ a place to store water

2. __I__ ten years

3. __F__ one hundred years

4. __B__ a place where people no longer live

5. __H__ the capital city of the Aztecs

6. __A__ waterways built by people

7. __J__ wide roads over water

8. __G__ the land and peoples under the control of a powerful nation

9. __E__ the largest city in the world

10. __C__ anything that makes air, land, or water unclean

A. canals

B. ghost town

C. pollution

D. reservoir

E. Mexico City

F. century

G. empire

H. Tenochtitlán

I. decade

J. causeways

(continued)

Part Two: Test Your Skills (25 points)

DIRECTIONS: Use the maps to answer the questions.

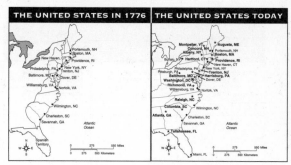

| Map 1 | Map 2 |

11. What states are on Map 2 but not on Map 1? __Maine, Vermont, and Florida__

12. What cities in Pennsylvania are on Map 2 but not on Map 1? __Harrisburg and Pittsburgh__

13. What city in Georgia is on Map 2 but not on Map 1? __Atlanta__

14. Where was the nation's capital city in 1776? __There was no national capital in 1776.__

15. Where is the nation's capital city today? __Washington, DC__

(continued)

Part Three: Apply What You Have Learned

DIRECTIONS: Complete each of the following activities.

16. **Short Answers (15 points)**
    Answer the following questions.

    a. List three types of disasters that can cause a place to change.

    Possible responses: earthquake, flood, hurricane, fire, oil spill

    b. List three types of technology people use today that most people did not have 100 years ago.

    Possible responses: television, fax, computer, automobile, video, microwave

    c. List three ways people in Mexico City can help lower the amount of air pollution in their city.

    Possible responses: closing factories that cause pollution, using special fuels

    that cause less pollution, having no-driving days, using public transportation

(continued)

17. **In Your Own Words (10 points)**
    Your teacher has asked you to write a history of your community. Tell in your own words the people you would talk to and the places you would go to get information for your report. Explain why you chose those people and places.

    Possible response:
    People might include family members, members of the local historical society, community officials, and other members of the community. Places might include the public library, the local historical society, the local museum, and newspapers.

ANSWERS

Individual Performance Task
Change Over Time

Towns and communities change over time. In this task you are going to make three bar graphs that show the changes in the number of people who live in three different places. After making your graphs, you will use the information to make conclusions.

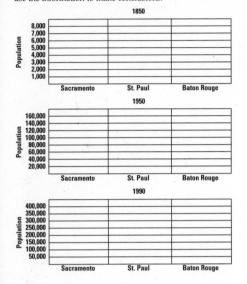

Step 1 Use the information in the table below to make three different population graphs on the grids on page 59.

Year	SACRAMENTO, CA Population	ST. PAUL, MN Population	BATON ROUGE, LA Population
1850	6,820	1,112	3,905
1950	137,572	311,349	125,629
1990	369,365	272,235	219,531

Step 2 After you have completed your graphs, answer the following questions.

Which city had the largest population in 1850?

Sacramento

Which city had the largest population in 1950?

St. Paul

Which city had the largest population in 1990?

Sacramento

Which city's population declined between 1950 and 1990?

St. Paul

What conclusion can you make about these cities and their populations? Possible response: Some cities gain population over time, and other cities lose population over time.

(continued)

Group Performance Task
Then and Now

Places change over time. In this task your group is going to make two maps. One will show an area of your community or an area near your school as it was ten years ago. The other map will show the same area as it is today.

Step 1 With your teacher's help, decide the area your map will show. It may be a part of your community, town, or city or the area around the school.

Step 2 Make a list of people you can talk to who will know about the area your map shows. This list can include school officials (principal, teachers, staff, custodians, bus drivers), parents and grandparents, community officials, and other citizens in the community. You may also want to visit your school library, public library, and the local historical society.

Step 3 Make a rough sketch of the area you have chosen as it looks today. Each member of the group should show this map to the people on your list and ask them how this area looked ten years ago. Write down their answers.

Step 4 Make a rough sketch of the area as it looked ten years ago. Go back to the people you talked with, and ask them whether the map is what they remember. The map may help them remember more information.

Step 5 Make two final poster-sized maps. On the map titles, include the dates they represent. Use labels to show the areas that have changed in the past ten years. Display your maps in a place where others can see them.